Also by Leslie McGuirk

TUCKER FLIPS!
TUCKER OVER THE TOP

TUCKER OFF HIS ROCKER

LESLIE McGuirk

Dutton Children's Books · New York

Library of Congress Cataloging-in-Publication Data

McGuirk, Leslie.
Tucker off his rocker / by Leslie McGuirk.—1st ed.
p. cm.
Summary: Trying to cool off, Tucker the dog takes a wild ride.
ISBN 0-525-46398-4 (hc)
[1. Dogs—Fiction.] I. Title.
PZ7.M4786235 Tv 2000 [E]—dc21 99-048163

Published in the United States 2000 by Dutton Children's Books,
a division of Penguin Putnam Books for Young Readers
345 Hudson Street, New York, New York 10014
www.penguinputnam.com
First Edition   Printed in Hong Kong
1 2 3 4 5 6 7 8 9 10

My friend Paul Galdone told me I should do a children's picture book about my dog, Tucker. He said, "He's off his Scottish rocker!"— and there was my title.
I dedicate this book to my sweet memories of Paul, who ignited this spark.

100° F

Tucker is a hot dog.
He needs to cool off.

Tucker off his rocker...

...and in front of the fan.

Tucker in front of the fan...

...and onto his skateboard.

Tucker on his skateboard
and under a gorilla.

Tucker under a gorilla
and into a taxi.

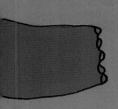

Tucker in a taxi and through a snowman.

Tucker through a snowman
and onto a flying carpet.

Tucker on a flying carpet
and behind a cloud.

Tucker behind a cloud
and under a parachute.

Tucker under a parachute and...

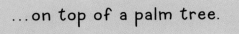
...on top of a palm tree.

Tucker on top of a palm tree
and above hula-hula dancers.

...and below a stork.

Tucker below a stork and onto a raft.

Tucker on a raft and next to alligators.

Tucker next to alligators
and over the water.

Tucker over the water
and onto a chariot.

Tucker on a chariot and over a bump.

Tucker over a bump and into the air.

Tucker into the air
and onto his skateboard.

Tucker on his skateboard
and up his driveway.

Tucker up his driveway and into his house.

Tucker in his house and onto his rocker.

 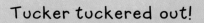

Tucker tuckered out!